A NOTE TO PARENTS

When your children are ready to "step into reading," giving them the right books—and lots of them—is as crucial as giving them the right food to eat. **Step into Reading Books** present exciting stories and information reinforced with lively, colorful illustrations that make learning to read fun, satisfying, and worthwhile. They are priced so that acquiring an entire library of them is affordable. And they are beginning readers with an important difference—they're written on four levels.

Step 1 Books, with their very large type and extremely simple vocabulary, have been created for the very youngest readers. **Step 2 Books** are both longer and slightly more difficult. **Step 3 Books,** written to mid-second-grade reading levels, are for the child who has acquired even greater reading skills. **Step 4 Books** offer exciting nonfiction for the increasingly proficient reader.

Children develop at different ages. **Step into Reading Books,** with their four levels of reading, are designed to help children become good—and interested—readers *faster*. The grade levels assigned to the four steps—preschool through grade 1 for Step 1, grades 1 through 3 for Step 2, grades 2 and 3 for Step 3, and grades 2 through 4 for Step 4—are intended only as guides. Some children move through all four steps very rapidly; others climb the steps over a period of several years. These books will help your child "step into reading" in style!

Library of Congress Cataloging-in-Publication Data
Awdry, W.   Happy birthday, Thomas!/W. Awdry.   p.   cm.–(Step into reading. Step 1 book)
"Based on the Railway series by the Rev. W. Awdry." Summary: Thomas the train engine thinks that all the other engines are too busy to help him celebrate his birthday, but he is in for a surprise. ISBN 0-679-80809-4 (pbk)–ISBN 0-679-90809-9 (lib. bdg.) [1. Birthdays–Fiction. 2. Parties–Fiction. 3. Railroads–Trains–Fiction.] I. Awdry, W. Railway series. II. Title. III. Series. PZ7.A9613Hap 1990 [E]–dc20 89-49649 CIP   AC

Manufactured in the United States of America   5 6 7 8 9 10

STEP INTO READING is a trademark of Random House, Inc.

Step into Reading

Happy Birthday, THOMAS!

Based on *The Railway Series*
by the Rev. W. Awdry

Illustrated by Owain Bell

A Step 1 Book

Random House New York

"Peep! Peep!"
Here comes
Thomas the Tank Engine.

Thomas and his friends
work hard every day.

Thomas does not want
to work today.
It is his birthday!
He wants a party,
with presents,
balloons,
and silly hats.

MEN
AT
WORK

But Sir Topham Hatt says,
"Henry is busy.
Gordon is busy.
James is busy.

You <u>must</u> work today,

Thomas."

So off Thomas goes
to his branch line.

Back and forth.

Back and forth.

He carries people.

He carries animals.

He carries wood.

He carries grain.

Thomas sees his friends
near the engine shed.
No one says,
"Happy birthday."

No one says a word
about presents,
balloons,
or silly hats.

At the end
of the day
Thomas heads home.

"Those engines did not look so busy to <u>me</u>."

Oh no!

A cow is in the way.

"Move!" says Thomas.

"Moo," says the cow.

20

"No, no, no!"
says Thomas.
"Not <u>moo</u>. MOVE!"

At last the cow moves.

Thomas is late.

Thomas is tired.

Some birthday!

Sir Topham Hatt opens the doors to the dark shed.

Thomas chugs inside.

Lights come on.
"Surprise!"
say all Thomas's friends.

"We were busy making a party for you!" says James.

It is a wonderful party.

There are presents,

balloons,

and silly hats to wear.

Happy birthday, Thomas!